The Phoenix and *The Butterfly*

Written by T. J. Jurgens
Illustrated by Bob Hobbs

Order this book online at www.trafford.com
or email orders@trafford.com

Most Trafford titles are also available at major online book retailers.

3D Modeling by Martin Hendenstroem

Printed in the United States of America.

ISBN: 978-1-4269-5691-1

Library of Congress Control Number: 2011905268

Trafford rev. 04/06/2011

 www.trafford.com

North America & international
toll-free: 1 888 232 4444 (USA & Canada)
phone: 250 383 6864 ♦ fax: 812 355 4082

I would like to dedicate this to my daughters Danielle and Ashley who have been a constant inspiration in my life. There couldn't be a prouder father. I love them both dearly.

It was early morning, and a beautiful green butterfly named Ashley was perched on a daisy, which was slightly bent over because of the butterfly's weight. She had lived a relatively sheltered life in a beautiful meadow that was covered in yellow, purple, pink, and white flowers. Ashley spent her days exploring the meadow and looking at all the different types of flowers, enjoying the variety of colors. During her explorations, she also came across red foxes, snowy owls, furry rabbits, blue jays, cardinals, groundhogs, and other animals.

On one particular day, as Ashley explored the meadow, she saw an animal she had never come across before. It looked like a bird, but the wings, feathers, and head were unlike anything Ashley had ever seen. Ashley looked closer and was amazed when she discovered that every feather on the bird was covered in a bright red flame. She also noticed that the head was bigger than the head on a normal bird and it too was surrounded by a red flame. Its wings were bigger than they should be for a bird of its size, and Ashley figured they might allow the bird to fly extremely fast. She also noticed that the bird's entire body was glowing, though she did not know why!

Ashley was drawn to the bird. She slowly flew closer and then landed on its wing. Something in Ashley's head told her that this creature was called a phoenix. Ashley decided to rest on the phoenix's wing because her own wings were tired. The phoenix then opened its wings to begin flying. All of a sudden, a brilliant red fire covered the entire phoenix. Ashley was very afraid because she thought the fire would burn her. However, after a few minutes, Ashley realized that the flame was not hurting her; in fact, the flame made her feel warm and protected.

Ashley was now hitching a ride on the back of the phoenix. The phoenix started flying faster and faster, higher and higher into the air. Ashley was now going at greater speeds than she had ever dreamed possible. She looked down and watched as the ground below got farther and farther away. The meadow that Ashley thought was so big started to get smaller as they flew higher. No longer were the flowers visible. The meadow now looked like a field of rainbows. Ashley also noticed that there were trees surrounding the meadow. As they went even higher, the trees became a sea of green. She then noticed a mountain with snow-covered peaks and saw that part of the mountain sparkled red.

Being so high up would normally have frightened Ashley, but the warmth of the phoenix's fire made her feel safe. Soon, she could no longer see any of the details on the ground below. Instead, she could see the curve of the earth, the different colors of the land, the oceans, and the occasional cloud. Knowing she could never reach these heights on her own, Ashley understood the great opportunity she had been given to view the earth from the wing of the phoenix.

Ashley now focused on where they were going because it was becoming too scary to think about how high they were. As the phoenix continued to climb higher into the heavens, Ashley noticed that the sky was no longer blue. It was now a black blanket speckled with brilliant shining stars. Ashley had never seen the stars this close before and was amazed at how sparkly they were. Ashley then looked toward the earth and could see the sun at the edge of the planet; it was a great big ball with hundreds of shades of orange and red. As they climbed higher, Ashley looked up at the moon. It was glowing like a million fireflies, and she could see its mountains and valleys.

As they climbed higher, the air got thinner and thinner. You see, as you get farther away from the earth, there is less air; that's why airplanes need to have their own air inside them when they fly. The phoenix was a very strong bird and did not need a lot of air to survive. Ashley, however, needed air just like you and me. The phoenix's flame kept Ashley warm and safe from the cold of outer space, but there was not a lot of air in the bird's aura. Ashley was not accustomed to being this high and started to fall asleep. As she slowly dozed off, a haze covered her thoughts and she began to dream about all of her adventures in the meadow far, far below.

The phoenix was flying so high now that they were no longer surrounded by the sky as we know it. Even though it was daytime, the stars were still visible. Ashley stirred and began to wake up. Through half-open eyes, Ashley gazed in utter amazement at the brilliance of the heavens now so close. Normally, the cold of space would have hurt Ashley, and the brightness of the stars would have been too much for her to look at; however, the flame that surrounded the phoenix was not a normal flame like that created by a campfire. This was a magic flame, and it protected the phoenix from the cold of space. The aura created by the flame made the phoenix almost invincible, and anything inside the aura was also protected. Ashley was safe from the coldness of space.

As the phoenix climbed, it looked down at the earth far below. This was the first time the phoenix noticed Ashley on its wing. The phoenix noticed that Ashley was half-asleep and understood that it was because there was not much air in the flame covering the wing. So the phoenix focused, and the flame around its left wing started to fill with more air. To Ashley's amazement, she started to breathe easier and then fully wake up. The phoenix has somehow helped me, she thought.

The phoenix knew that shortly it would break through the upper atmosphere. At that height, there would be no air and no heat. The bird knew that it would take a lot of energy to maintain the protective aura so high above the earth. The phoenix also knew that if the flame went out when the two of them were that high, it would be very dangerous for both of them. Yet, the phoenix was a powerful bird and considered itself invincible. It had grown cocky over the years and believed nothing could hurt it. So the phoenix continued flying higher and higher into space, and as it did, the air grew colder and colder. To the phoenix's surprise, it was starting to get tired, and it felt its energy slowly running out. The phoenix realized that it had flown too high, so it began the process of turning around. You see, the phoenix valued life above all; it was a creature of great compassion and wanted to maintain its flame in order to protect the life of the butterfly. The phoenix was using almost all of its energy to maintain the flame and the protective aura that kept the butterfly alive.

The phoenix was traveling faster than a jet plane, so turning around took some time. Before the phoenix realized it, the two of them had broken through the upper atmosphere, and the stars were so close that Ashley imagined reaching out and touching them. By this time, the phoenix was extremely tired, and the absence of air and the coldness of space suddenly hit the majestic bird like a million gallons of ice-cold water. The phoenix lost focus, and for a split second, the fire went out. The phoenix faltered. Then it started to fall!

When the phoenix's flame went out and it began to fall, the protective aura no longer surrounded Ashley. The beautiful stars and glowing moon had now been replaced by darkness, as Ashley realized she could no longer breathe. She instinctively grabbed on to one of the phoenix's feathers. Ashley started to shiver and then shake because the freezing temperatures of space were no longer held at bay by the phoenix's aura. Panic set in as Ashley held on for dear life. She was so cold, and she could not breathe. The poor little butterfly was very scared.

The phoenix was now in free fall and was getting closer and closer to the earth. The air was becoming thicker and warmer, but the phoenix did not notice this because it was almost asleep. You see, it had used most of its energy to fly into the upper atmosphere. The phoenix was extremely tried and was almost asleep as it fell towards the ground. However, she was aware of the butterfly's feeling. Ashley was very afraid and panicky. With the air being so much warmer now, the phoenix was able to shake off the initial shock of being so high, and like the explosion of a billion suns, its flame reignited. As warmth returned to the butterfly, she started to realize where she was and that this bird of fire had just saved her life.

Ashley looked down under her tiny feet and realized that one of the phoenix's feathers was missing. When the phoenix's flame went out, the sudden change in temperature had caused one of the feathers to fall out. Without the feather, the phoenix surely would have perished in the cold of outer space because each and every feather plays a role in creating the aura. In the absence of even one feather, the phoenix's flame is not as strong, and the cold of space can find its way in. The presence of Ashley's wings had shielded the area where the phoenix's feather no longer existed; the butterfly's wings had acted as a makeshift feather, protecting the magnificent bird from the bitter cold of space.

The phoenix slowly started to descend, and once again Ashley felt the warmth of the sun and the cool air rushing through her wings. Being out of the cold of space, the phoenix was able to focus on healing itself. The missing feather slowly started to grow back; first the thin shaft of the brilliant feather appeared, and then the rest of the feather grew in. It was a crimson red feather and was covered in flames, just like the rest of the feathers on the phoenix.

N ow they were on the ground, and the phoenix no longer needed its flame, so it allowed it to slowly go out. Ashley flew off of the phoenix and landed on the daisy that she had been perched on earlier in the day. Once again, the daisy bent from her weight. Ashley realized that even though she was an extremely small creature, she had an incredible impact on her surroundings. Her presence had saved the phoenix, and that made Ashley feel proud.

So remember, like the butterfly, no matter how small you are or how big the world feels to you, you make a difference. You are special and important, just like the butterfly. You make a big difference in this world, and the world is a better place because you are in it. Love surrounds you.